The Adventur

Pop Fantastic

and his

Autistic Superpowers

www.pop-fantastic.com

The Adventures of

Pop Fantastic

and his

Autistic Superpowers

By David and Amy Fox

Illustrations by Merve Terzi

For
Ollie Pop, Antonia Pancake, Harri Rabbit

and all of our very special friends

Thank you to everyone who helped make this book possible

It was an early Monday morning and though the sun was still sleeping, Pop was wide awake. Pop always woke up early, before anyone else in the house. He could never sleep as long as his mum, dad and sisters did.

Pop watched as the sun started to peek through his curtains, this was the time when Pop would usually start getting ready for school, but this Monday was different. There was no uniform to put on, no snack to prepare and no bus to wait for.

This Monday was the first day of the summer holidays.

Now most children love the holidays, and so did Pop, well, he loved the idea of holidays, but Pop found that no school and no routine, left him feeling worried, confused and even a little scared.

Pop liked school, it was good to know what was going to happen that day.

He started to feel sad, so he did things that usually made him feel better. He watched his favourite cartoon, read his favourite book, he lined up all his toys exactly how he wanted them, but still Pop was not happy.

"I don't like this feeling", thought Pop. And as a tear began to roll down his cheek, his little sister Pan ran into his room.

Pop loved Pan, he loved to chase and tag her, he loved her big smile most of all…. but he did not like her loud voice.

"Look Pop, look!" Pan shouted. Pop covered his ears.

"Sorry Pop", Pan whispered, "but look what I've made for you."

In her hand was a picture; Pan loved to draw pictures, she had drawn it for him the night before.

"It's for you!" Pan explained, as she handed it to Pop. "It's to make you feel happy. It's a place that I dream of sometimes, with amazing creatures and people I love."

Pop looked carefully at Pan's picture. Under a cool blue sky, Pan had drawn what looked like a little village surrounded by bright green fields. Behind it were mountains that shone like crystal and there was a leafy forest near the bottom.

Although Pop liked the picture, it hadn't made him feel much better.

"Ah thank you Pan, now please, I want to be on my own",
said Pop.

"Who's awake so early in the morning", asked Mum,
"is it my Pop and Pan?"

"I've drawn Pop a picture, to make him smile" said Pan.

"What a lovely thing to do" said Mum "let's put it up on
your wall Pop."

"Ok, but then I need to be alone" sighed Pop.

That night, before Pop went to bed, he looked at the
picture on his wall and remembered what Pan had said
about it being "a happy place". Still thinking about the
picture, he climbed under the covers and fell fast asleep.

The sound of a car door woke Pop with a start.
Most people would not have heard it, for it was very quiet,
but Pop had very sensitive ears.

The sun was almost at his window when Pop remembered
that today would be another day of feeling worried.

"I don't want to feel sad again", thought Pop as he
climbed out of bed.

Just then the sun streamed in through Pop's window and
lit up Pan's picture with a flash.

Suddenly the picture started to sparkle and gleam as if
alive with magic.

A bright light shone out from the edges of the paper and
seemed to wrap itself around Pop, a warm and comforting
feeling surrounded him like a big hug. He closed his eyes
and felt himself being pulled towards something strange
and new.

Slowly Pop's eyes opened. He was standing on soft green
grass under a pale blue sky. As he looked around he saw
mountains in the distance and what looked like a small
village at the bottom, just like in Pan's picture. Was he still
asleep? Was it a dream? Was he inside the picture?

Whatever was happening, Pop realised he wasn't feeling
worried anymore. He felt happy and rather excited now.
He could hear birds singing as they flew through sky and
when he listened carefully he could just could make out
a high-pitched whistle, it sounded very much like a train.
Pop loved trains and the sounds they made.

All of a sudden, Pop heard a loud and piercing cry. It wouldn't stop and seemed to be getting louder. Pop found the noise quite painful, so he covered his ears with his hands. Pop looked around, searching for whoever was making the noise. From out of nowhere, a little girl was running towards him, she was crying, she was crying very loudly.

The little girl stopped when she reached Pop, she could see that he had covered his ears.

"Oh, I'm so sorry", she sobbed, "I didn't mean to scare you, it's just, it's just...", she struggled to stop the tears, "I've lost Charlie", she sighed as she slumped on the grass.

"Is Charlie your friend?" asked Pop.

"Yes", replied the little girl, "My best friend. He's my pet and he's been missing all night. I've been searching and searching, and I don't know where else to look."

Pop could hear what the girl was saying but still he kept his hands firmly over his ears.

'It's ok", the little girl said, "I promise I won't cry so loud, did the noise hurt your ears?" she asked quietly.

Pop nodded his head and then moved his hands down by his side.

"I hate loud noises and you gave me a shock."

"I really am sorry" said the girl wiping the tears from her face. "My name's Bo, I just don't know what I'll do if I don't find my Charlie."

"I'm Pop", Pop said.

"I get sad too when I lose things, once I lost my favourite toy for two days, then I found it in Pan's bedroom, she's my little sister, I felt so cross but also very happy that I'd found it".

'I could try and find your friend if you want, then that will make you happy again too!" exclaimed Pop excitedly.

A big smile spread over Bo's face. "Really, you would help me? Oh, thank you so much. I don't know where to look though, I've already been to all the places I know Charlie likes."

"What does Charlie look like?" asked Pop. "Oh, he's very cute, he has the softest orange hair and the biggest brown nose, he has a fluffy orange tail and six tall legs."

"Six legs?" asked Pop feeling confused

"Yes", said Bo, "six, like all snugglings."

"Snugglings? I've never seen a snuggling before." said Pop excitedly.

"Really?" asked Bo, "they're really friendly, especially Charlie. Snugglings make the loveliest purring sound when they're happy, but when they're scared or hurt they make a rather funny whistling noise, but it's very quiet so don't worry."

"A whistling sound? I can hear a whistling sound, I've been hearing it since I got here." smiled Pop

"Really? can you hear it right now?" asked Bo in surprise.

"Yes, it's coming from over there", Pop said as he pointed towards the mountains.

"I can't hear it", said Bo. "You must have amazing hearing, I wish I had a super power like that."

Feeling proud, Pop's cheeks began to turn red. He laughed and was just about to start flapping his hands (something Pop liked to do) when Bo grabbed his arm.

"Come on, what are we waiting for? You can lead us straight to him!"

And off they ran with Pop's super-hearing leading the way.

As the whistling sound grew louder, Pop knew they were getting closer. They ran and ran until they suddenly came to a fork in the road. Pop saw that one path wound up towards the mountains where the sun was bright, and the air was clear. The other sloped down into a dark and wooded place where the air felt damp and the thick leaves on the trees blocked out the sun.

"It can't be that way", said Bo, "I don't think Charlie would go down there, he's quite scared of the dark woods."

Pop listened carefully to make sure where the noise was coming from.

"It's this way", Pop said nodding his head towards the gloomy path. 'The noise is coming from down there."

Bo was nervous. As Charlie always followed the path that led up to the mountains, she had never walked through the dark woods before. There hadn't been a reason to go that way and she didn't really want to now. But Bo trusted Pop's ears and so she gripped his hand. Pop didn't usually like holding somebody else's hand, but now he felt a little nervous, so he held on tightly. Pop felt safer too.

A little further down the path, Bo looked down; there were paw prints in the mud. Bo knew straight away that they were Charlie's.

"Pop look, you were right", she gasped. "Charlie must have come this way, I'd recognise those paw prints anywhere!"

Just as Bo started to relax, she noticed another set of prints. They were bigger than Charlie's and it looked like they had been made at the same time.

"I think I know why he came this way", whispered Bo. "I think he was being chased."

"Chased by what?" asked Pop.

"I don't know", Bo admitted, "but something else has definitely come this way too. Can you still hear him?"

"Yes", Pop replied, "we're close now, the noise is coming from just over there."

Pop started to walk faster, so did Bo and soon they were both running through the woods until Pop shouted, "Stop!"

They looked around until Pop spotted a big brown nose peeking out from a hollow log. It was Charlie.

"It's ok Charlie, it's me, you're safe!" cried Bo. "Whatever could have been chasing you?" she wondered.

At that moment Charlie leapt out from inside the log and straight into Pop's arms. Pop was startled.

"Wow! He must really like you", laughed Bo. "I told you snugglings were really friendly!" Pop liked the feeling of soft hair, he used to like stroking his mum's hair when he was really little, it made him feel calm. Now, running his hands through the softest hair he had ever touched, Pop felt a wave of happiness wash over him. "I like Charlie too", said Pop.

As they retraced their steps back to the fork in the road, Pop asked Bo if she knew what had chased Charlie into the dark woods, and left its footprints behind.

"I'm not sure", replied Bo, "although I know there are creatures that live on the other side of these trees. They always hide from us though, so nobody really knows what they look like. Some people say they have enormous wings and can fly as fast as the wind and I've heard others say they have huge paws and can run for days without stopping. We don't know if they're dangerous or not, but knowing that they've been so close to our village makes me feel worried."

Pop could see that Bo looked scared. He knew that feeling and didn't like it, so he reached for her hand to make her feel safe.

As their fingers met, the light of the sun as it started to set, shone down on Charlie's face.

Charlie, the soft haired snuggling, purred, and as they came out of the woods he began to run, hopping from leg to leg with joy. Bo smiled and joined in giggling.

Watching this, Pop felt a rush of happiness and he ran after them flapping his hands in delight. He ran so fast he felt as though his feet weren't touching the ground and when he looked down he saw that it was true. His feet weren't touching the ground at all! HE WAS FLYING!!!

"How are you doing that?" shouted Bo from the ground below.

"I don't know!", laughed Pop "it just happened when I flapped my hands!

Wheeeeee!"

"Wow Pop, you're fantastic. You're Pop Fantastic!" yelled Bo.

Up Pop went, climbing higher and higher, flapping and giggling as he flew.

"I'm flying I'm flying", he sang.

As he turned towards the setting sun, Pop began to feel that same warm and comforting hug. He closed his eyes and felt himself being pulled into something safe and this time familiar.

As his eyes opened, he watched the orange and red of the sun fade into the cool blue of his bedroom walls. He was home. He had just caught his breath when his sister Pan, ran into his room, pointing at her painting.

"Oh, Mum did put it on the wall", she grinned. "Do you really like it Pop?"

"Yes", replied Pop, "I like it very much and I'm going to look at it all the time. You were right Pan, it is a happy place." he said with a smile.

After dinner, Pop sat in front of his T.V.

"Bed time", shouted Mum, "Have you brushed your teeth?

"Yes Mum", replied Pop, although he hadn't yet, he was still thinking about all the wonderful things that had happened that day. He couldn't believe that he had flown through the air. He crossed his fingers and hoped that it hadn't been a dream.

He smiled as he thought about the new friend he had made. Bo had been so nice to him, he hoped he would see her again.

As he climbed into bed feeling calm and content, he remembered the creatures Bo had talked about, the ones that lived beyond the dark woods, the ones that had chased Charlie. Bo seemed to be scared of them, but not Pop, he was excited. He wondered if he would get to see one the next time he went there... He would go there again, wouldn't he?

Pop felt so tired he could hardly keep his eyes open, but as he glanced at the picture on his wall one last time, he hoped with all of his heart that the morning sun would bring with it another fantastic adventure.

Would you like your child to join Pop on his next adventure?

For a chance to **NAME YOUR VERY OWN CHARACTER** in the upcoming **2nd** book in the Pop Fantastic series please subscribe at:

www.pop-fantastic.com/subscribe

School **Worksheets** to accompany this book can be downloaded from our website:

www.pop-fantastic.com